Where's My Share?

for
John, Helena,
Thomas, Patrick
and James

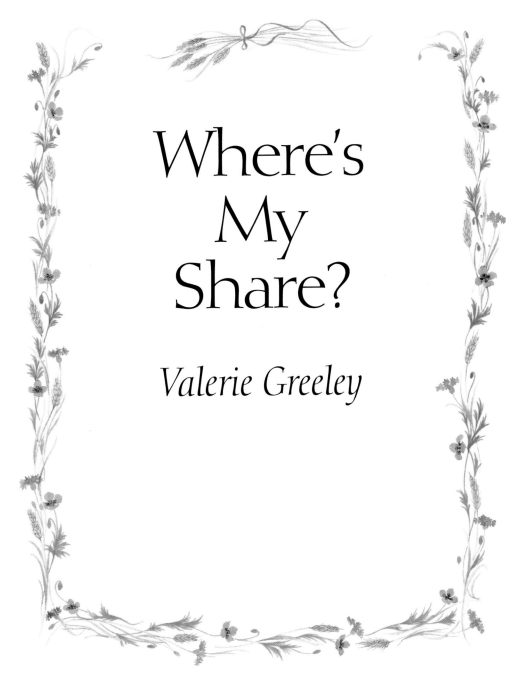

Where's
My
Share?

Valerie Greeley

Macmillan Publishing Company
New York

What's in there?

A loaf of bread.

Where's my share?

A mouse took it.

Where is the mouse?

In her house.

Where is her house?

In the forest.

Where is the forest?

Covered in snow.

Where is the snow?

The sun melted it.

Where is the sun?

Ripening the wheat.

Where is the wheat?

Milled into flour.

Where is the flour?

Baked into bread.

Where's my share?

The inspiration for this story was the rhyme "What's in there?" from *The Oxford Nursery Rhyme Book* by Iona and Peter Opie.

Copyright © 1989 by Valerie Greeley
All rights reserved. No part of this book may be reproduced or transmitted in any form or by any means, electronic or mechanical, including photocopying, recording or by any information storage and retrieval system, without permission in writing from the publisher.
Macmillan Publishing Company
866 Third Avenue, New York, NY 10022
Printed in Hong Kong
First published in 1989 by
Blackie and Son Limited
London, England

10 9 8 7 6 5 4 3 2 1

Library of Congress Cataloging-in-Publication Data
is available.
ISBN 0-02-736761-4